Kerry's Treasure Stick

Written by Jillian Powell

Illustrated by Javier Joaquín

Collins

Who's in this story?

Listen and say

Jane

Kerry

Peter

Ms Goody

Paul

Rose

The children were at the beach. Ms Goody gave everyone a stick and a bucket.

"Why do we need sticks?" asked Jane.

"To make a story stick," said Ms Goody. "A story stick can tell us about a place."

"Find nice things to put on your story stick." said Ms Goody. "Put them in your bucket, too."

Kerry wrote her name in the sand.

"No, Kerry," said Ms Goody. "You don't write with your stick."

"Sorry!" said Kerry.

"I'm digging for treasure!" said Kerry.

"You don't dig with your stick, Kerry!" said Jane.

"Look! I've got some seaweed for my story stick," said Peter.

"And I've got this pretty shell," said Jane.

"The seaweed and the shell are nice, but I'm looking for treasure," said Kerry.

"Look! I've got a big rock for my story stick," said Paul.

"You can't put that on a stick," said Peter. "This pebble is better."

A bird flew past Jane and Rose.
"Look!" said Jane. "This feather
is fantastic!"
"Can I have it?" asked Rose.

"Look here," said Ms Goody. "This wool is from the sheep on the farm!"

"I like that," said Rose. "Can I put it on my story stick?"

"Yes," said Ms Goody.

"What have you got?" Paul asked Peter.

"I've got some grass," said Peter.

"I've got a pink flower," said Paul.

"Kerry," said Ms Goody, "are these for your story stick?"

"Oh no," said Kerry. "I'm looking for treasure for my story stick."

"Wow, look at this rope!" said Peter.
"Can I have it, Kerry?"

"Yes," said Kerry. "I don't want it.
I want treasure."

"What's this?" Rose asked Ms Goody. "It's beautiful."

"That's green glass from the sea," said Ms Goody.

"It's pretty, but it's not treasure," said Kerry.

"Kerry, it's time for lunch," said Ms Goody. "You haven't got any things for your story stick."

"There is treasure here, I know there is," said Kerry.

The children have lots of things for their story sticks.

"What a lot of beautiful things,"
Ms Goody said. "Let's go back to school and make our story sticks."

"Let's go, Kerry," said Ms Goody.

Kerry was sad. "I haven't got any treasure," she said.

"Oh dear," said Ms Goody.

Then, Kerry looked down. What was that in the sand?

"Look at this," Kerry said to Ms Goody.

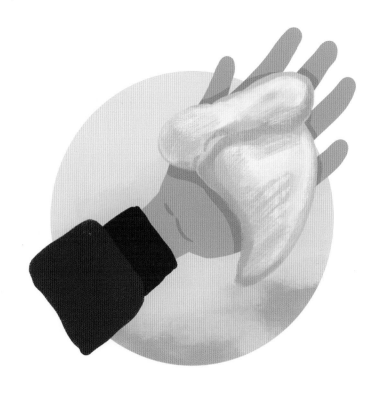

"It's a fossil of a shark's tooth,"
said Ms Goody. "It's very old!"

"Can I use it for my story stick?"
asked Kerry.

"Oh yes," said Ms Goody.

Kerry showed the tooth to her friends.

In school, the children made their story sticks.

"Which is your favourite story stick?" asked Ms Goody.

"Kerry's stick!" answered the children. "It's a treasure stick!"

Picture dictionary

Listen and repeat

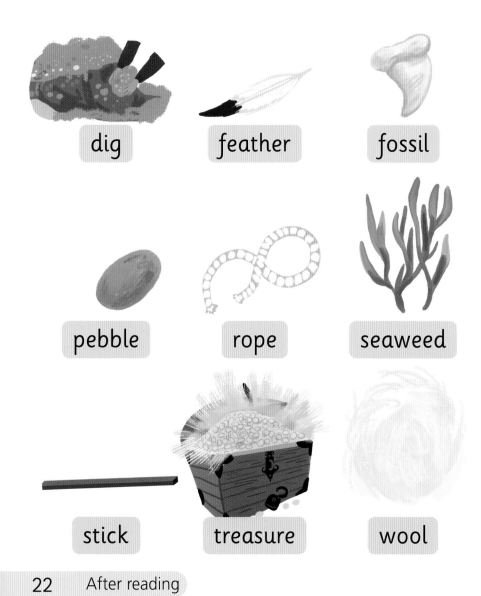

dig

feather

fossil

pebble

rope

seaweed

stick

treasure

wool

1 Look and order the story

2 Listen and say

Collins

Published by Collins
An imprint of HarperCollins*Publishers*
Westerhill Road
Bishopbriggs
Glasgow
G64 2QT

HarperCollins*Publishers*
1st Floor, Watermarque Building
Ringsend Road
Dublin 4
Ireland

William Collins' dream of knowledge for all began with the publication of his first book in 1819.

A self-educated mill worker, he not only enriched millions of lives, but also founded a flourishing publishing house. Today, staying true to this spirit, Collins books are packed with inspiration, innovation and practical expertise. They place you at the centre of a world of possibility and give you exactly what you need to explore it.

© HarperCollins*Publishers* Limited 2020

10 9 8 7 6 5 4 3 2

ISBN 978-0-00-839693-0

Collins® and COBUILD® are registered trademarks of HarperCollins*Publishers* Limited

www.collins.co.uk/elt

British Library Cataloguing in Publication Data

A catalogue record for this publication is available from the British Library.

Author: Jillian Powell
Illustrator: Javier Joaquín (Beehive)
Series editor: Rebecca Adlard
Commissioning editor: Fiona Undrill
Publishing manager: Lisa Todd
Product managers: Jennifer Hall and Caroline Green
In-house editor: Alma Puts Keren
Project manager: Emily Hooton
Editor: Matthew Hancock
Proofreaders: Natalie Murray and Michael Lamb
Cover designer: Kevin Robbins
Typesetter: 2Hoots Publishing Services Ltd
Audio produced by id audio, London
Reading guide author: Emma Wilkinson
Production controller: Rachel Weaver
Printed and bound by: GPS Group, Slovenia

MIX
Paper from
responsible sources
FSC™ C007454

This book is produced from independently certified FSC™ paper to ensure responsible forest management.

For more information visit: **www.harpercollins.co.uk/green**

Download the audio for this book and a reading guide for parents and teachers at www.collins.co.uk/839693